If GOD is a king ......
that makes me a Princess

Written By Loretta A. Morman
Illustrated by Natalie Marino

xulon PRESS

If God is a King, That Makes Me a Princess!
by Loretta A. Morman

Printed in the United States of America

ISBN 9781498461061

www.xulonpress.com

Hi. My name is Victoria, but my family and friends call me Vicki.

Sometimes my mom and dad call me "Queen" after Queen Victoria when I'm being bossy.

I tried to get them to let me change my name to Elsa because she was a princess and so am I!

I know, I know, you probably think I'm being silly, but really I am a true princess.

You see, I go to a Christian school called Grace Christian Academy, and in our class, we have been learning about all of the jobs that God has to do for us.

God really has a lot of jobs. I just don't see how he does it.

I mean he has to

Heal us,

Forgive us,

Take care of our needs,

Protect us from bad stuff,

Save us and

Rule us.

My teacher and my parents always tell me that I am a child of God, which sometimes confuses me because I already have a mom and dad.

But they say we are all children of God.

Once we believe that God's son Jesus died for all of the bad stuff we do, which are called our sins, we become a child of God.

Pretty cool right?!

My parents also told me that since we are God's children, we come from a royal family!

I didn't know what that meant until one day in class, my teacher said that God is known as the "King of Kings."

Well since he is a King, and I am his child, then that must make me a princess!

Oh, and did I tell you that I have my own princess crown?

See! I told you I was a princess! Let me tell you how I got it.

Well one day at school we had a talent show and I signed up to read one of my poems.

I just love writing and drawing. It is really fun!

I even drew some of my friends in my poem! They were really happy, but back to my story.

So there I was standing in front of my class, and I was a little nervous.

I cleared my throat and then began to read my poem to the class:

TODAY'S LESSON

$$\frac{3}{4} + \frac{1}{4} = \frac{4}{4} =$$

$$\frac{3}{7} + \frac{2}{7} = \frac{5}{7}$$

$$\frac{7}{12} - \frac{5}{12} =$$

$$\frac{2}{9} + \frac{5}{9} =$$

$$\frac{8}{9} + \frac{4}{9} =$$

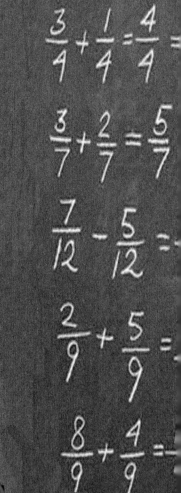

If God is a King, That Makes Me a Princess

By: Me, Vickie

"If God is a King That Makes Me a Princess

I'm so special that He made me different than all of the rest

I'm not like Cinderella, Elsa, Tiana, or Belle

God made me unique so I'd have my own story to tell

I'm one of a kind, you cannot buy me at stores

I have my own gifts and talents that no one can ignore

My smile, my hair, and even my skin were all specially made for me to live in

When I look in the mirror, I'll tell you what I see

I see a beautiful princess looking back at me

If God is a King, if that's really true

Then that means there is also a prince and princess, in all of you, too

The End."

I finished reading my poem, and the entire class got up and cheered.

Then I noticed my mom and dad snuck in the back of the room to surprise me! Boy was I excited!

I rushed from the front of the room to give them a great big hug.

Then my dad reached from behind his back to give me a gift...and guess what it was?

A crown! A beautiful silver crown all for me.

He placed it on top of my head and kissed me on my forehead.

Then my mom hugged me and whispered in my ear, "You will always be our little princess Victoria."

The next day my parents let me wear my princess crown to school!

All of my friends wanted to try on my crown and they kept asking me to say my poem over and over again.

We all began to say it together and even made it into a song!

My teacher was really proud of me for being a leader.

She said that I helped all of my classmates with knowing how special God made us!

Well, I hope that you know just how special God made you!

Read my poem again and again so you will know that there is really a prince or princess inside of you, too!

"If **God is a King, that Makes Me a Princess**"

If God is a King, that Makes Me a Princess
I'm so special that He made me different than all
of the rest

I'm not like Cinderella, Elsa, Tiana, or Belle
God made me unique so I'd have my own story
to tell

I'm one of a kind, you cannot buy me at stores
I have my own gifts and talents that no one can
ignore

My smile, my hair, and even my skin were all
specially made for me to live in

When I look in the mirror, I'll tell you what I see
I see a beautiful princess looking back at me

If God is a King, if that's really true ...

Then that means there is also a prince and
princess in all of you, too

CPSIA information can be obtained
at www.ICGtesting.com
Printed in the USA
BVOW07s2227090316

439779BV00002B/2/P